This book is for Olimpia, my big little "thing".

And a big thank you to Pata who is never far.

B.A.

English edition first published 2019 by order of the Tate Trustees
by Tate Publishing, a division of Tate Enterprises Ltd,
Millbank, London SW1P 4RG
www.tate.org.uk/publishing

First published in French as *La Gigantesque Petite Chose* © Autrement 2011
This English edition © Tate 2019
English translation © Daniel Hahn 2019

A catalogue record for this book is available from the British Library

ISBN 978 1 84976 645 6

Distributed in the United States and Canada by ABRAMS, New York
Library of Congress Control Number applied for

Printed and bound in China

Beatrice Alemagna

The Big Little Thing

One summer's day, the thing came by.
It slipped right past Sebastian's feet.

A little girl tried to catch hold of it,
as if it were a fly.

The crocodile lady waited for it for many long months,

standing at her front door. But she never saw it.

Some people can't recognise it,

even when it's right before their very eyes.

Someone walked straight past it
in the middle of a rain shower.
Just for a minute or two, no more than that.
But a minute was enough.

During the summer holidays,
it slid beneath somebody's hand.
A slight crackling . . . and then that was it.
That was all.

An old gentleman found it inside a snowflake,

in the deep cold that came from distant lands.

For just a moment, he thought he was little again.

A lot of children, when they grow up,
discover they can no longer find it
in the toy box or in the cookie jar.
"Oh well," they say to themselves.
"It's probably for the best."

Hard to believe, but some people are actually afraid of it.
They shut their doors,
move far away from their neighbours
and build high walls.

One day, perhaps as a joke,
the thing hid itself inside a tear
and filled a man with nostalgia
for the old days.

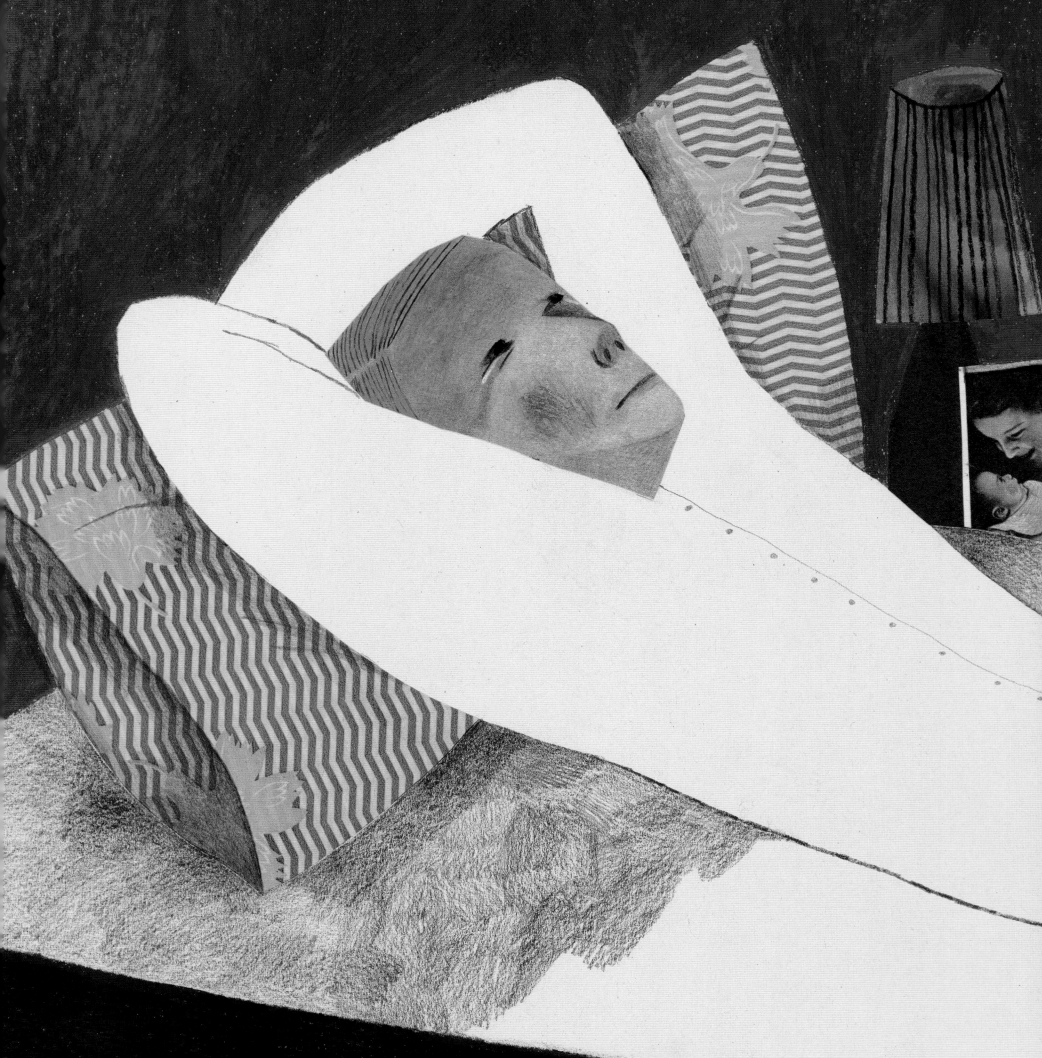

Some of us find it in familiar smells,

or in tender glances,

or in other people's arms.

Others chase after it constantly.
Sometimes they try to buy it with money,
or to shut it up in a box.

But it cannot be kept.
It only ever passes through.

Swirling like a leaf,
it comes to rest
on somebody's shoulder . . .
then quickly flies away again,
vanishing in an instant.

And there it was, nestling
right under our noses,
but once again
we failed to spot it.

This tiny invisible thing,
which is also a great big thing,
that somebody once named

happiness.